I0518261

Sinnerman

A Regina Grant Mystery

By Ngozi T. Robinson

I AM Publications

Sinnerman

Copyright © 2022 by Ngozi T. Robinson

All rights reserved. No part of this publication may be reproduced, distributed, or transmitted in any form or by any means, including photocopying, recording, or other electronic or mechanical methods, without the prior written permission of the publisher, except in the case of brief quotations embodied in critical articles and reviews and certain other noncommercial uses permitted by copyright law. For permission requests, please contact the publisher.

I AM Publications

(617) 564-1060
contact@iampubs.com
www.iampubs.com

Cover art by Soda Khan

ISBN: 978-1-943382-18-7

Murder Most Foul

Summer nights in Washington, DC are the best. The city has an exciting pulse to it and comes alive in a special way. There's a life and excitement that can be a joy to get lost in. But nothing could cover up the stink of what was to come.

A McLaren pulls up to the curb. A man in a slick suit gets out and paces along the stone steps of a church. He looks at his watch and paces harder. As he looks down the road for signs of someone approaching, a figure in a ski mask steps out from behind a column and draws closer. The black steel of a revolver glints in the light from the street lamps. Few appreciate the joy of a revolver these days.

The shot reverberates against the stone steps and brick buildings. Those moments of sound seem to last forever. The man falls down the stairs. His limbs lie at odd angles. A pool of blood gathers underneath him and spreads out from an exit wound in his chest. Cowards shoot you in the back.

Police litter the scene. They don't all need to be here, but once a call like this goes out, everyone wants a piece. There's talk among the detectives that the victim is everyone's favorite cult leader, James Hamerson, founder of The Society for Ageless Wisdom. To have him gunned down on the steps of a church he would have never stepped foot in has many people asking questions.

The evening worship service inside the church had been in full swing at the time of the shooting. Church members spill out of the building and onto the steps, mingling with police and barely making room for the body. It is hard to tell who is who.

Agent Dellers exits the back seat of a car and tells the driver to wait. Dellers is a tall, chocolate, and well-built drink of water. There is something about his smile, though, that never seems to reach his eyes.

He walks to the center of the chaos and shouts in a thunderous baritone voice, "Who's in charge here?"

"I am," a tall redhead retorts as she turns to size up the man that goes with the voice. Her mouth, which is ready to unleash a dressing down on him, slackens, and her jaw drops as she sees the FBI badge he holds up to her sour face. There is literally nothing local law enforcement hates more than hotshots who parachute in and step all over everything.

"Feds, huh?" She walks alongside the agent as he heads to the body. "So, it really is him? We figured a bigwig would probably show up."

Officers flank a woman holding the leash of a very scary-looking dog. She stands near the body and looks terrified. Forensic photographers light up the night with camera flashes as they record the scene. They illuminate the woman's face in a way that makes her look haunted, or maybe hunted. There is something about that face that sticks with you.

"Who is she?" Dellers asks, drawn to her.

"Oh. She's the eyewitness."

"Really?" She suddenly becomes even more interesting.

"She saw the killer, and the killer saw her." The redhead gives him a knowing look, but he isn't paying her enough attention to notice.

"What's her name?" Dellers pulls out a notebook and pen.

"Sarah Williams."

Dellers scrawls the name down and looks at her.

"Sarah." He tries the name out on his tongue and decides he likes the way it feels.

Dellers mumbles something to the redhead and heads towards the witness. The redhead watches as he walks away.

"Jerk doesn't even know my name." The redhead walks back to the other detectives, trying to forget her authority was just superseded by someone who hadn't even looked at her.

"Ms. Williams," Dellers flashes his badge. "Why don't you tell me what you saw?"

"He...he saw me." Her voice was thin and brittle. "The killer saw me! I don't like being out here with all these people. I am in danger!"

Dellers reaches for her arm to guide her to a car, but the Rottweiler by Sarah's side barks and bares his teeth.

"Sorry." Sarah tightens her grip on the dog's leash. "Genghis just wants to protect me."

Dellers knows the dog is going to be a problem.

"I was only trying to suggest we could get you into a police cruiser and out of all this madness. Would you like that?"

"Why, yes, thank you. I apologize for being so high strung, but he saw me. You have to protect me!"

"Believe me," Dellers said with a generous smile. "I won't let anything happen to you."

But he didn't see the pair of eyes in the crowd that had been tracking Sarah Williams since the shots first rang out. Those eyes had seen it all.

Day at the Office

Regina Grant wakes up with Reginald's butt in her face. Every morning is like this. Her cat is a jerk.

"I will feed you when I get up, Reginald."

She turns the other way and wills herself to go back to sleep. Reginald stands on her head. She guesses it's time to get up.

Scooting across the short distance between her bed and the stairs, Regina heads down to the first floor. It has only been a few months since she bought her tiny house on wheels, but she is getting the hang of things and settling into the swing of things well.

The idiosyncrasies of Tiny Tina, as she calls her place, have stopped surprising her. Checking her propane and water sensors, she is relieved to see she has more than enough for a nice, long shower. She had already had her shower turn cold because she ran out of propane on more than one occasion and had learned to plan ahead. And whenever her septic guy comes to drain her black tank, she drops everything. He is the most important man in her life. If only he were single, she pines.

Looking in her bathroom mirror—it's the only room in her tiny house that looks normal-sized—she fixes the white collar around her black shirt and instantly feels at ease and on task. Reverend Grant is on the job.

She touches the lock on her front door to lock it with her fingerprint and walks the 50 feet to her church. As she walks the church perimeter as usual, she sees someone still sleeping on the front steps. Walking over, it is hard to see who it is because of all the layers of worn and tattered clothes.

"Ricky, late night?" The pile of rags moves and seems to morph into a person.

"Hey, Lady Pastor! What's good?"

"Well, the word of God, but you already know that. You're usually over in the park by now. What's up?"

Stretching out his left leg, he moans. "Knee's acting up. Taking it slow this morning."

"Ooh, be careful. You need anything?"

"Could I get five dollars, Pastor?"

"Ricky, you told me never to give you money because you are just gonna drink it away. But breakfast is on me. I'll even bring it out to you since your knee's hurting; just don't get used to me waiting on you hand and foot."

"You got pancakes?"

"Today's French toast, I think."

"Oh, good. Thanks, pastor."

"And be sure to come into the cooling center before it gets too hot. I hear it's gonna be a scorcher."

Regina takes the long way to her office, stopping by the basement to say hi to everyone at the free community breakfast, and to put in Ricky's order. Mondays were her favorites. Coming back up the narrow staircase, she takes time to appreciate the old brick building. It had stood the test of time; it and the church were preparing to celebrate their 100th anniversary later this year. She had only been here for one of those years, but the church's excitement was contagious.

Walking past the admin office, she put the mug of tea in front of the church clerk.

"Today's blend is peppermint, lemongrass, and spearmint. I didn't add any sugar, so sweeten it to your tastes."

"Pastor, I was kidding when I bought the Royal Treatment voucher you submitted for the fundraising raffle. You don't have to do this."

"Ms. Pring, it is my pleasure and duty to be your humble vassal for the next," Regina looks at her watch, "23 hours and 58 minutes. So drink up. Those for me?" Regina looks at the envelopes in her hand.

"Just prayer mail. I was about to put it in their ministry box."

"Well, give me a few. I'll answer them."

"Mmm-hmm." She hands two envelopes to Regina instead of three or four because she knows Pastor bites off more than she can chew. "So, Ms. Jens called. You didn't mention the flower dedication in service yesterday, and we forgot to update it in the bulletin, so no one knows. She's very upset."

"Seriously?" Regina rolls her eyes and sighs. "Fix it."

"The flowers were for the one-year anniversary of the passing of her unborn child. You remember baby Mary."

"Shoot." Regina's heart drops. "So, we're wrong, and it matters. I'll call her. We'll figure something out. Set up a time for us to meet. Did we send flowers?"

"I wasn't sure how to recognize the date. We didn't observe stuff like this before, but you put it on the observation calendar, so we sent a card."

"Weep with those who weep, Ms. Pring. Well, let's apologize and make it right, or at least less wrong."

"I'm on it."

"Where would I be without you? I'm in my office until a lunch meeting if you need me. And this is for you." With a flourish, she places a gift card to Slade's, Ms. Pring's favorite chicken place, on her desk. "Just part of the vassal service, milady."

Ms. Pring smiled, and her older, round face beamed. "If you insist."

Regina walks down the hall past the library and trustees' office to her office at the end. She presses her code into the keypad, opens the door, and sticks the doorstop under the door to announce she is open for drop-ins. Dropping her messenger bag and purse on her desk, she walks over to her fancy tea maker and presses the brew button. She dreamily anticipates her cup of ginger oolong that will mark the start of her workday.

Regina pulls out her iPad and opens her news app. It's been a week, but the murder of James Hamerson still dominates the headlines. The Society for Ageless Wisdom had been controversial enough *before* the murder. Now it was infamous. America was still trying to figure out whether it was a wholesome, loving religion or a predatory cult, and so was Regina.

She reflects on how easy it is to manipulate people sometimes. She knows well the incredible sway she has over some because of her position and the power of her ministry. If she had made different choices, perhaps she could have been James—leader of a rogue Christian offshoot that vowed to get back to basics.

But somewhere along the line, it had gone wrong for him and The Society of Ageless Wisdom. Mired in scandal after scandal, questionable teachings, the ostentatious exalting of the founder, his lavish lifestyle compared to the simple lives and slavish devotion of his followers was all too much. Had it all been a con from the beginning, or were she and James merely a few decisions apart?

The call to ministry is not something Regina takes lightly. She really is trying to fulfill God's command to love her neighbor as herself. It consumes her, but not so much that she can't see the dangers of and the trespasses done in the name of faith. Regina had always been uncomfortable around people that seemed like they were following her more than they were following the LORD. As a pastor, she often saw folks at their most vulnerable, desperate moments. She knows the power she holds. James Hamerson showed her how easily the work could be corrupted. She has to find out what had happened to him.

The A Train

Regina Grant smiles from ear to ear. She is never on time, but, for once, she is actually going to make her train as scheduled. She is early, even. This is a major stop of the trip and there is extra time for boarding as freight and other items get loaded onto the cargo cars. Regina watches the handlers load a very loud and angry looking Rottweiler into one of the cargo cars. It snaps at them like there is a score it can't wait to settle. Regina is glad she only has a cat. Reginald is a jerk sometimes, but mostly harmless.

She makes her way to the sleeper car, scanning for the number of eligible men—the numbers still weren't in her favor—and boards. Finding cabin 12, the Red Cap puts away her luggage. She tips him and gives her thanks. Regina waits for him to leave before she struts around her small room like she is a bigwig. The days when she had to travel standing room only, and be grateful, were not so far behind her that she couldn't appreciate her recent turn of events for what they were, a blessing.

She had convinced her hosts to spring for the overnight Palmetto Silver Service train from D.C. to Florida instead of a flight. Regina has never been on a fancy train before and thanks God for every little amenity, especially the private bathroom. The place feels like home already.

Regina comes back to reality when her watch vibrates to alert her to a call. She grabs her phone and smiles as she answers.

"Pastor!"

"Pastor."

They laugh because it is still funny.

"My dear daughter in the ministry, I am so excited we are going to have you preach the first night of our revival this weekend. The people are excited. I hope you have something for them. What's your sermon title?"

There is a long pause.

"You haven't written it. This isn't your little church of 30 or 40, this is the big leagues. You know you're the only woman on the panel. I expect you to be ready."

"I'm always...well, usually...Oh, I'll be ready! I know this is a chance to take my ministry to the next level. Don't worry, I'm not gonna blow it. Hey, you trained me; it's got to work out."

"Don't disappoint me, daughter. The fields are so white..."

"And the laborers are few," she recites dutifully. "See you soon, Pastor Croning."

Regina settles in and starts to work on her sermon, which always puts her in another zone, so at first she doesn't notice the sound of a key turning in her door as the knob turns back and forth. Finally, Regina notices and wonders if this is how she dies. She is far too dramatic.

Creeping up to the door, with her own terrified eyes, she can see the knob jiggling. Regina grabs her hard copy Bible with grim determination, lifts it overhead, and with the other hand opens the door, determined to put up a fight. A dowdy older couple seems frightened and confused when Regina opens the door looking menacing.

"Oh. Oh. No, excuse me. Is this room 18? We're the Palmers. What are you doing here?" The woman's voice sounds nosey.

Regina lowers her raised arms and loosens the death grip on her Bible. "No, this is not room 18. This is room 12."

"I told you, Gregory. That's why the key wouldn't turn." The woman taps his shoulder in rebuke, then looks at Regina apologetically. "They all look the same."

Regina points to the numbers beside her door. The Palmers look at them as if they have never seen numbers before and scurry off towards room 18. Hopefully.

Regina rolls her eyes and shuts her door. It was better than being murdered. Squeezing her shoulders together and then releasing, she focuses on relaxing and enjoying her time.

'I wonder if this is how it was in the old days,' Regina ponders as she enters the seated dining car for dinner service. There were actual tablecloths on the tables for two and four in the car as waiters walked to and fro. But she bets they won't have French toast, she regrets. There should be more places that serve breakfast all day.

She scans the room for single men and identifies four, though none she would want anything to do with. A sigh escapes her as the search continues.

"May I help you?" An inquisitive host smiles at her.

"Yes, one for dinner."

"Hmm...This is a crowded seating. Do you mind if I seat you with someone?"

"Oh, not at all," Regina lies. She hopes the young woman doesn't plan to seat her with the drunk man in the corner. Some people can't handle their liquor.

The young woman leads her to a table for two where a pale brunette woman sits looking over the menu. As she sits opposite the lady, Regina notices a skittish quality to her. Smiling, Regina decides not to speak as she settles into her seat.

'Is this neurodiversity, shyness, or meanness?' Regina wonders as the hostess hands her a menu. 'Would I have been better off with the half-sleep drunk?'

Her stomach greedily rakes over the menu options and hunger threatens to put her in a tizzy. Good food is a delicious gift from above. The chicken pot pie with handmade crust is screaming for her to pick it, so she does. Regina could do worse than have a silent dinner companion. She forces herself to stop fantasizing about her dinner or it will never live up to expectations.

"I'm sorry," her suddenly not-so-silent dinner guest says. "I didn't mean to be rude. Hello, how are you?" She has put the menu down and looks like she wants to have a conversation. Regina doesn't mind at all.

"Oh, no worries! It's nice to meet you. I'm Regina Grant."

"I'm Mary Stanners. Um, what are you having for dinner? I got the chicken Marsala."

"Hi Mary, I got the chicken pot pie. Are you going all the way to the end, like me?"

"Oh, I don't know." Mary rubs the back of her neck and looks away.

"You don't know? How strange. You must be a first-class adventurer then." Regina gets excited about the stories she may ply from the woman over dinner.

"Oh?" Mary laughs. "No, it's nothing like that. I just travel a lot. It's hard to keep up with where I'm headed. This time, I'm going to Florida to visit my nephew."

"Sounds like a first-class adventurer to me," Regina says optimistically. "Tell me, where is the most amazing place you've been to this year?" She wishes she could travel more.

"Well," Mary steeples her hands together as she thinks, "It would have to be this little cabin in the woods by a stream." Her eyes get a dreamy look.

"Sounds like something special."

"Oh, I know." Mary laughs. "It doesn't sound like much. Sometimes it's the combination of the place and the company that makes for sweet memories."

"Oooh, does Mary have a boo?"

"A what?"

"A love interest. Tell me more about this special company."

"Do you think you can ever make it work with an ex?"

"Nope," Regina says as she crosses her arms. "Never, never, ever." Her features and body language softens. "That may have something to do with the fact that I'm still single."

Laughter bubbles up at the table as Regina and Mary share appetizers and personal histories.

"So you're a pastor? Wow! Why do I suddenly feel like I've been called to the principal's office?"

"Ex-Catholic?"

"Guilty."

"Called it. I don't have a Heaven or Hell to put you in, so how about you not feel guilty or like you have to be something you're not?"

"Deal."

Regina likes the amiable smile Mary has, now that she has warmed up a bit.

A passenger walks by and tips over Mary's glass of red wine and it spills onto her sleeve. That shirt looked expensive.

"Oh dear! I...would you excuse me? I'm going to my cabin to see if I can rinse this out before it sets. If they bring my dish, just have them leave it for me."

Regina watches her leave, unaware that three other sets of eyes are also tracking Mary. A tall man in a black leather jacket leaves the dining car. Is it all the cop shows she watches, or is the way he holds himself slightly off because he's wearing a gun holster that grabs her notice? Regina can't decide.

It is only after Mary has left the compartment that Regina sees she has left her purse at the table.

Leftovers

The chicken pot pie is so good, it helps keep Regina from giving in to her worries about Mary. As the dessert cart rolls by, she picks a classic—strawberry cheesecake.

"Mary Stanners?"

An older man in a train uniform holds an envelope as his eyes scan the diners. Regina raises her hand, and the man dumps the letter in it before she has a chance to explain Mary is not in the car right now.

Regina has to get Mary's purse and the envelope to her. When she signs the bill for dinner, she sees on the bill for the table that Mary has already charged her meal to her room—number 34. She takes Mary's things and heads to room 34.

Before she can knock on Mary's door, the train lurches back and comes to a grinding halt as the interior lights flash off and on. Regina makes her way to the end of her car and sees passengers milling about outside. Not a single thought about how she would get back up and into the train troubles Regina as she hops down.

The night is hot and sticky. Train workers check the wheels of the train with flashlights. What are they looking for? Regina doesn't want to know, but suspects she needs to. A train worker passes her.

"Hi! Why are we stopped?"

The man stops walking as if Regina has ruined his entire life plan. He turns his body to face her, but his head is still looking ahead into the middle distance. He sighs, and Regina wonders if she should walk over into his line of sight to make the point that you look at people when you talk to them.

"A passenger pulled the emergency brake. Said they saw someone fall from the train."

"Are you telling me any Tom, Dick, and Harry can *actually* stop a train?"

"Yes, that is what I am telling you." The man turns away and walks farther down, directing a weak flashlight back and forth over the train wheels.

Regina can't tell where they are. It seems like the middle of nowhere. Walking away from the train, she takes a bright yellow brochure from her purse and secures it on the ground with two rocks.

"I hope I don't have to come back for you," Regina whispers to the paper.

The path seems longer on her way back than she remembers. The conductors try to make her feel bad for taking the same liberty half the other people on the train did in getting off, but she pretends not to care. Regina has other things on her mind and returns to Mary's room.

Mr. And Mrs. Palmer pop out of room 18 in their nightwear. Regina thinks it figures that they are party poopers.

"Oh, hi! Did you see? Did you see? The train stopped, almost like it was a heist or something! We heard they didn't find a body, so why would someone stop the train?"

"That's the million-dollar question," Regina answers as she tries to move past them. They step out farther in the hallway to block her.

"Well, what do you think happened?"

"I don't know, but I intend to find out." She peels herself away from the Palmers before they can extend the conversation.

No one answers when she knocks on the door to room 34. Regina tries the handle, because she can't leave well enough alone, and it opens. The room looks like someone tossed it. Clothes are strewn everywhere. Mary's blouse with the wine spill is in the bathroom's small sink, soaking.

Regina decides to go through Mary's purse and open the envelope. She feels a sense of time draining away and hopes she can find Mary before it's too late. There is nothing in the purse, almost literally. There is no phone or wallet, just a pair of sunglasses, a Nintendo Switch handheld gaming system, and a picture of Mary and a young boy. Her son? No, it must be the nephew she said she was going to visit. She reads the note in the envelope. The handwritten scrawl is barely legible. *"Give me what I want."*

This time, Regina doesn't let her reading deafen her to the sound of a key turning in the door's lock. A disembodied hand holding a gun comes into view at the door. The gun looks too long, then Regina realizes it has a silencer on it. 'This is how I die,' she thinks.

Regina stands up and raises her hands in surrender as the older man in the train uniform that handed her the envelope steps into the room. "Alright, Sarah Williams, where is what I'm looking for?" The man's tone is hard, like he is used to getting his way.

"Who? *Who* is Sarah Williams?" Regina is scared and confused.

"Don't play games with me. You have what I want, and I mean to get it, Sarah."

"For the last time, who is Sarah Williams? I'm Regina Grant, and I don't know what any of this is about."

"Nah, nah, nah. I don't care how many aliases you use. Regina Grand. Mary Stanners. Whatever. They're all you."

The man comes further into the room. He makes gestures with his gun hand. That's how Regina knows he's not a trained killer. People who are trained never take their aim off their target, at least that's how it is on the cop shows she watches.

"What about Mary Stanners?" Finally, the man mentions a name she recognizes. "Yeah, that's you. Your little moniker," the man laughs to himself. Apparently, he thinks he made a joke. "Look, you're in the room assigned to you. You answered when I called your name in the dining cart. Stop evading. You won't like it if I have to get rough."

The calluses on his knuckles let Regina know he is serious.

Suddenly, the drunk from the dining car appears at the door, peering through the slivered opening at them.

"Oh, Mary! I'm so glad you're here!" Regina looks with relief in the drunk's direction.

The man with the gun doesn't buy her tremendous acting.

The drunk walks up behind him, raises a wine bottle and hits him in the head as hard as he can. He hits the ground like a sack of potatoes and the gun clatters as it falls out of his hand.

The Chase

Regina tries to figure out which of the three of them is more dangerous. She keeps her hands raised. The drunk—well, he doesn't seem drunk now—closes the room door and lays the man out. He rifles through the man's pockets. There is no sign of a phone or wallet. The drunk looks up at her. "If he watched TPN Faith Network, he would have known you weren't Sarah Williams. Nice to meet you, Rev. Grant."

"You know me?" Regina's head continues to spin from new information.

"Yes. I like to keep track of what's going on in the world. So what is the minister who says we should love everybody doing in a missing woman's room?"

"Somebody better tell me what's going on or I'm going to scream."

"Calm down. No need to get loud. I'll explain everything, as much as I know anyway, but first we've got to get rid of this guy before he wakes up."

"He's still alive?"

"Yes, I'm no killer!"

"So what do you mean 'get rid of him?'"

"Let's throw him off the train. We're going slow now. He'll be fine. Grab his legs and let's get this done."

Regina crosses her arms. She will not help him. Then she thinks about how she would explain this unconscious man with a growing lump on the back of his head in somebody else's tossed room. He had been ready to kill her. She uncrosses her arms and picks up the feet, helping the drunk throw the man off the train. She supposes she will find out if she did the right thing later.

They return to Mary's room.

"Alright, so who are you really? I can't keep calling you 'drunk guy' in my head." Regina folds her arms and stares at him.

"My name is Sam Wallers, though my ex-wife might agree with your name for me. I'm a reporter. Sometimes I cover the religion beat, that's how I know who you are. This story I'm investigating now could be my Pulitzer. I've been following Sarah for two weeks now. Wait. Sarah was the one eyewitness to the murder of James Hamerson? The cult leader shot dead on the steps of Methuen Baptist Church. Remind me where you pastor, again?"

Regina gets caught because she is never as slick as she thinks she is. Her head hangs down for a moment at the feeling of being busted. She raises her head to face the music.

"Yes, James died on the steps of my church while I was preaching inside. And she is the only witness. I want to get to the bottom of things, so I've been sort of investigating."

"Sort of investigating? Is this what you went to school for?"

"I've got to find out who killed James Hamerson, and right now that means we have to figure out what happened to Mary—I mean Sarah."

Sam looks Regina over, assessing her. He decides to trust her, at least for now.

"I know it happened at your church that night because I was there. A lead I had led me to James. He said he was ready to tell the truth about his Society for Ageless Wisdom. He said he had proof that would destroy the organization he started. We arranged to meet at your church. He said it was a place no one would expect him.

"I was late. By the time I got there, the place was swarming with cops and people. Maybe, if I had been there on time, I could have done something."

The guilt on Sam's face was a burden Regina recognized all too well. She leaned forward and clapped her hand on his back.

"Well, you're doing something now. We have to tell someone about this."

Sam's body fills with purpose, and he straightens himself. "First, let's make absolutely sure that she's not on this train. I'll check the front of the train and you can check the back. Let's meet back here in ten minutes."

"Let's go."

Scanning dozens of faces as you pass by without looking like you're doing that is harder than Regina thought it would be. She finally makes it to the cargo compartments, where she sees a man she saw loading containers at the train station.

"Ma'am, we try not to have passengers in this compartment."

"Oh, hi. I saw you when we first departed. I didn't realize you were on the train and not at the station."

"Yes ma'am, going on 35 years I've been with the company. Been on this line for 13 of those years." The older man's chest swells with pride.

"Well, amen. Dedication is hard to find these days. Since you know so much about trains and this line, let me ask you, where exactly were we when the train had its unexpected stop?"

"Hmmm," the man accepts the challenge. "Do you know what time that was?"

"8:40pm. I checked."

"We left on time at 6:12." The man does a little light math with his hands and fingers. "Probably right in the middle between Petersburg, VA and Rocky Mount, NC. Rocky Mount is coming up next."

"You know, that's the closest to one of those, 'If a train leaves at 6:12 at fifty miles an hour, when will it reach Timbuktu' type of questions I have ever had to ask in real life?"

"Our math teachers would be proud." The man holds up a hand, and Regina high fives him. Thanking the man for his help, she rushes back to Mary's room. She has important information to tell Sam.

For the third time on the train, Regina hears someone turning the doorknob as she waits inside Mary's room. This really is how she's going to die. She creeps near the door.

"Sam," she whispers, "is that you?"

Grabbing a glass shard from the broken wine bottle and making up her mind to stab with it if she needs to, she opens the door. and it's Sam. But something is wrong with his face. It's all twisted up. He collapses into her arms, but he's too heavy for her and she has to let him fall to the floor. Regina sees a small red hole in his chest. He has been shot dead.

All the King's Horses and All the King's Men

After checking for a pulse, Regina confirms the sad truth of Sam's death. She decides to bless the man before she brings down a world of trouble on her head. She looks up the prayer for the dead that Catholics say, since she sees a crucifix around his neck, and recites it over the body.

Loving and merciful God,
we entrust our brother to your mercy.

You loved him greatly in this life;
now that he is freed from all its cares,
give him happiness and peace forever.

The old order has passed away;
welcome him now into paradise
where there will be no more sorrow,

No more weeping or pain,
but only peace and joy
with Jesus, your Son,
and the Holy Spirit
for ever and ever.

Amen

"I have a feeling you'll enjoy that heavenly wine with Jesus. Hope you made it."

She closes his eyes, shaking her head to think of how many times she has done this. Standing up, Regina goes to tell someone in charge what's happened.

＊

"So you're just alone in someone else's room who no one can find, with a dead man, and you have no idea who shot him? Oh, this just keeps getting better and better."

Sheriff Tillis needs a win. This just might be the kind of break that could get him out of this two-bit town. The only thing it has going for it is that the train still stops there. But there are other kinds of beauty to find in small towns that Tillis refuses to see.

Regina sits in the small interrogation room at the two-bit sheriff's office. She doesn't think much of this sheriff, but is determined not to be the next Sandra Bland, so she is bending over backwards to be pleasant.

"And you still claim you didn't hear the shot that killed him, huh?"

"I did not hear a shot. And I'm sure by now the other passengers have confirmed that they didn't hear a shot either. You could ask them."

"Oh, I'm not interested in them. I've got my eyes on the one who was in the room with the dead man. So why don't you go over things one more time, nice and slow."

A tall, chocolate drink of water enters the room, and Regina loses focus. She loves tall, chocolate drinks of water.

"Hold on there," the man says, "I'd like to hear that myself." He looks at Sheriff Tillis like he stepped in something. "That will be all; I'll take it from here."

"Now hold on a minute, boy. This is my county, and I'm in charge. I'm not gonna have someone else tell me what to do, especially not some..." he looks at the badge the man has put in his face, "...federal agent." Sheriff Tillis gives up and exits the room. "Well, come on, Emma," he gestures to his deputy. "I guess it's time to see about Miss Jones' cat." They leave together to catch up on small town business.

The chocolate drink introduces himself as Agent Frank Dellers and takes a seat across from her.

"Agent Dellers, you have lost the only witness to the murder of James Hamerson, who was supposed to be under your protection. I'd say this is a very serious situation." Regina's tone is full of censure.

"How do you know about Sarah?"

"Who? Oh, Mary. I met her on the train. It looks like the victim, Sam, and I weren't the only people acquainted with her on the train. I sure wish you had done your job, Agent Dellers. Where is she?"

Apparently, Regina is only afraid of local law enforcement, but feels bold around FBI folks.

Dellers' eyebrows raise.

"Listen Ms..." he pulls out his notebook and starts flipping through the pages.

"Reverend," Regina says with emphasis as she crosses her arms. "What are you going to do about Mary?"

"Who? Oh, Sarah. Listen Reverend, that is our job and we are handling it."

"Are you going to keep handling it like you did tonight?"

Dellers puts his hands on his hips and looks her up and down. "Why do you care, anyway?"

"Why don't you? A woman is missing. She's the only one who saw James' killer. His blood cries out to me! Where is your sense of urgency? You are supposed to stand for justice, and you promised to protect her. Someone has to stand for these people!"

Dellers stands up and towers over Regina. She does what she always does when men try to exert power over her by standing—she stares at his crotch, which is at eye level. Dellers shifts uncomfortably and moves from standing directly in front of her.

"Reverend Grant, if I were you, I would get back on your train. I don't want you in this town or thinking about Sarah anymore. You'll do that if you know what's good for you."

Regina stares at him with a deadpan expression to show she is neither impressed nor afraid. Somewhere in her brain, her fears are running with their hair on fire shouting, 'The FBI are going to disappear us!' She should be afraid, more afraid of the agents than she is of Sheriff Tillis, but right now she can only think about Mary.

Hours off-schedule, the train finally departs from Rocky Mount, NC. Regina watches it leave from the station platform.

"If I know what's good for me? He doesn't know me at all."

Society Town

"Pastor Croning, how are you?" Regina pours on the charm in her voice.

"Reverend Grant, I'm good! Calling to tell me you've written your sermon and to give me the title?"

"Not exactly. Something's come up on the trip I have to take care of. I'm not on the train anymore. I'll be there on time, with a sermon, just not early."

Croning sighs. "Grant, you have a nasty habit of being late. That's why we wanted you here early."

"I promise I'll be there on time," Regina sends up a small prayer that she's not lying to her mentor. "There are some loose ends I need to tend to first."

"We'll see, Grant. Don't forget, you're going to have a whole church waiting to hear what you have to say. Don't let us down."

Regina's phone flashes "Call ended" and she registers she has just been hung up on. It is not as if she enjoys being late, but things always seem to get in the way. This time, the thing is a missing woman who could crack a murder case wide open.

Inside the train station, Regina finds a detailed map of the area. Her eyes scan it until she finds what she is looking for—Browning, Virginia. It is at the midway point between the two stops where the train's emergency brake was pulled. It is also the headquarters of James Hamerson's Society of Ageless Wisdom.

Regina knows the names and locations of a bunch of communes. It's a hobby. Occasionally, she threatens to run away to one. The Society of Ageless Wisdom had been on her short list until the stories about gross financial mismanagement had come out. Was that what James Hamerson wanted to talk to Sam Wallers about?

None of it will come to light if she can't find Mary. What are the odds a train would make an unexpected stop near Hamerson's headquarters right around the time when Mary disappeared? It might be a long shot, but Regina decides to pursue it.

She is disappointed when she discovers there are no ride-hailing services in Rocky Mount. It would have probably cost a fortune, anyway. The station agent helps her find a local bus heading out to Browning first thing in the morning. Rocky Mount's one hotel is ridiculously priced, and it is already after midnight, so Regina sleeps sitting on a bench in the train station and tries to ignore the fact that the station agent has a very 'I'm going to chop you up in my basement' vibe going on with his beady little eyes. It is not a restful night.

The bus ride shows Regina some beautiful landscapes. Lush southern trees lined the highway. There are even wildflowers on the dividing grounds. It is almost enough to melt her and make her forget she's searching for a missing woman and trying to solve a murder. She cannot forget the sight of Hamerson's blood running down her church's front steps. She remembers what she is after and focuses.

Browning, VA, or 'Society Town', as the locals call it, looks like nothing special to Regina. You won't know that one of the country's most controversial cults owns this town—lock, stock, and barrel. The Society for Ageless Wisdom swooped in 15 years ago and saved the local mine. The Society took that appreciation and turned it into adoration. For the first time, the commune came to the people.

'This is the town that James built' is commonly heard by locals. They are all his followers with what seem like laudable goals for a community of faith. James Hamerson taught them to live simply, seek knowledge, and forgive. Regina really admired the Society. He changed so many lives for the better. It is hard to tell when it turned from a loving community of believers to a cultish worship of the man himself.

Regina still can't decide what kind of man Hamerson was—a fraud playing the long con or a charismatic faith leader who let things go too far. Now, she will never have the chance to talk with him and make her own assessment.

Regina knows she is a city girl, but thinks she is not overreacting about the strangeness of Society Town. Everyone sort of dresses the same—they seem to adopt the frontier era for inspiration, so they all look to be a bit in shambles. She has read that almost all the businesses and most of the residences are owned by members of the Society. Perhaps that explains why they all have the same haircut.

As soon as she gets off the bus, Regina sees that blending in will not be a possibility. She regrets having worn pants because all the women and girls are wearing dresses. Are people actually gawking at her? She decides she will feel no guilt for her fashion choices. How much could she ever really blend in, anyway?

So, she does what she loves to do—smile and live her best life, even though others are uncomfortable with her. Regina smiles at the faces turned towards her with judgment in their eyes, as if they're old friends. She waves to folks because she can't leave well enough alone.

Making her way through the little town—it had a village feel to it; should she call it a hamlet—she found the motel. Is it the only one? The doilies and cat figurines everywhere tell Regina she would rather stay anywhere other than here. The '80s wants its kitsch back. Maybe she can wrap things up before she has to stay here tonight. There is a tall, willowy woman sitting behind a desk whose cat sweater identifies her as the owner.

"Well, hello there." 'Am I being too folksy?' Regina wonders.

The woman lifts her eyes from the book, and her brown eyes stare for a few long moments.

"Wait a minute," she says in a one-note voice. "I know you." Narrowed eyes continue to peer at her. "You're...Reverend Regina Grant." She turns around and shuffles through some papers. A bright blue book in her hand, the lady turns to Regina and holds it out to her. "Would you sign my copy of your book?"

It's Regina's turn to stare dumbfounded. This is not what she expects in Society Town, or anywhere, really. This lady may be the one person who bought her book, and it's one of Hamerson's flock.

"But aren't you a 'Society girl'?" Regina realizes too late that she shouldn't have used the term that the papers bandy about when digging into the Society for Ageless Wisdom. "I apologize. You're you, not a term I read somewhere. And this must be a tough time. I'm sorry for your loss." Regina tries to make up for her thoughtlessness with empathy.

The innkeeper's entire demeanor changes. She slumps and suddenly looks defeated.

"All the people that have been here since his death, you're the first to offer condolences. Thanks. It is a hard time. I'm Lilith."

"It's so nice to meet you, Lilith. A lot of people have been through? I wonder if you saw my friend, Mary." Regina pulls out the picture of Mary with her nephew that she found in Mary's purse. "We talked about meeting here yesterday or today, but I haven't been able to find her. Has she checked in here?"

The woman takes the photo and looks at it for a long time. "I surely haven't seen her, but I will keep a lookout for her." She speaks solemnly, as if making a vow.

Regina looks at the woman. The conversation should be winding down, but Regina can't help herself.

"So," she pauses, "what did you think of the book?" She doesn't realize she's holding her breath.

The lady taps the spine of the book. "I like your ideas about grace. I think our James would have liked you."

Regina doesn't know how to take that because she hasn't decided who "our James" really was.

"I'm glad you liked it. Say, where's a good place to get breakfast?"

"You going like that?" She eyes her pantsuit suspiciously.

"I thought I was."

"No, no, it's fine. Go out and take a right. Down two blocks is Eddye's Cafe. Tell them Lilith sent you." She hesitates for a moment. "I wouldn't tell them you are a minister."

"I wasn't planning on it. And thanks for the advice."

"My pleasure." There is another pause. "Do you think we'll make it? You've probably seen a lot more churches have problems and suffer losses than I have. Can we make it without our James?"

Regina sees tears in her eyes as she contemplates a life without her spiritual father. What makes a church survive or go under? Nothing and everything. She has no idea how to answer that question, so she walks to the opening in the counter separating them and opens her arms. Lilith falls into them and cries like she's been waiting for a hug her whole life.

Sometimes you're exactly where you're supposed to be.

Sheriff Jerome

Eddye's Cafe looks homey, but the people are frosty, it seems to Regina. When she walks in, about a dozen eyes turn in her direction and pin her where she is for inspection. They all see the pants. They can't not see the pants. Why are they red on top of everything else? It is never a good feeling to be weighed and found wanting.

"Lilith sent me," she says in a confident voice and forces herself to plaster on a smile.

The waitress behind the counter pours a cup of coffee and sets it in front of an empty chair. It looks like that is all Regina is going to get by the way of welcome. She doesn't even drink coffee.

"Hi all." Regina settles into her smile and her seat to begin digging in. Looking at all the nearby plates, she finds one where she can identify everything. "I'll have what he's having."

The man eating from the plate she points to looks at her. "You got good taste." His laughter livens the place up.

That laugh is the only chink in the town's unfriendly-to-outsiders vibe she needs to worm her way in. "Hey, maybe you've seen my friend Mary. She's another city slicker, but I bet she'd eat you under the table." Regina pulls out her picture of Mary.

The man takes the photo, and the waitress leans over the counter to look at it as well. "She can't out eat me. Look at that little waist! But now let me see. I think I have seen her."

"You have? Where?"

"At the feed store last week."

Regina's face falls. "Oh, that couldn't have been her. She only got here last night."

A chirpy laugh fills the air as the waitress laughs. "Who'd you see her with, Elvis? Not again, Cletus." Other customers join in on the laughter.

"You know that was an honest mistake," Cletus says in a loud, annoyed voice.

It's too late. The crowd will have their amusement.

Angling her way back into the conversation, Regina speaks up. "I want to have time to take some nature photos. That's why I'm here. Which way do I go to get near the train tracks? That area is so picturesque."

Cletus and the waitress share a look. "That's our James' Lot. We're not to go near it. You shouldn't go, you'll get in trouble."

"James' Lot? What's that?"

Cletus looks down, and the waitress shrugs. "Who knows, but no one goes there." They seem to be trying to stare Regina down.

"What do you think is there?"

"Why bother?" The waitress moves down the counter to fill other customers' coffee cups.

Cletus leans toward Regina and says curtly. "Aliens," before straightening back up and getting back to his food.

Her jaw actually hangs as she takes that in.

The walk to the train tracks from Browning takes longer than Regina thought it would, and she wishes she had better shoes for hiking. The wildflowers are beautiful, and she snaps photos of them, regretting that she can't compose more artistic pictures. Finally, she finds the train tracks. Walking beside them, Regina finds the bright yellow piece of paper she had left by the tracks. That means that her suspicions were correct; the train had definitely stopped near Browning last night.

Why would Mary have gotten off the train right where the man she had seen murdered had a compound? Regina eyes the very clear signs ahead that warn folks not to enter private property. So, this is James' Lot. She is feeling defiant.

A beat up four-by-four that says Browning Sheriff in faded letters pulls in front and startles her. 'It's a good thing I wasn't sneaking,' she thinks. The first thing Regina notices is the tall, good looking, cinnamon-colored hunk of a man that gets out of the truck. No ring, hallelujah Lord.

Holding her hands up, she sings, "But I didn't shoot the...,"she leans over to see the name on his truck," Browning Municipality Police Department," and hopes the sheriff gets the reference. He doesn't, but not everybody has to like Bob Marley, Regina concedes.

"When the folks at Eddye's told me some lady was going to walk out in this isolated area alone, I thought they were lying. But now I see they were telling the truth. It's a little hot to be wondering around in strange places, don't you think?" The sheriff puts his hand on his gun belt, and Regina thinks, again, 'This is how I die.'

"It *is* hot."

Her words hint at her being her own woman and not being afraid of a walk into the wilderness at the height of summer. Regina saves her sarcastic comments. Now back in the hands of local law enforcement, she has no desire for something "unfortunate" to happen in the Browning Sheriff's custody. But the sheriff is still hot.

He sees her looking at the private property signs.

"Don't do it," he warns.

"What do you think is in there?" Is it the answer to her Mary problem?

The sheriff stands between her and the "No Trespassing" sign. "I don't ask, and they don't tell me. Let me give you a ride back into town." He walks over to the passenger side of the truck and opens the door, showing that his words are a command, not an option.

Regina squints her eyes so that he looks less handsome. She kicks at rocks by her feet all the way to the door. There she receives a delightful surprise. A five- or six-year-old, if her age-guessing skills are accurate, sits in the truck kicking his feet against the center console. It's a good thing the truck is well-worn and probably invincible to the wicked devices of bored kids.

"Why, hello! Are you the deputy?"

The boy has a toy badge on his shirt and he sticks out his chest to display it proudly. "I'm Jimmy. I'm my daddy's best deputy." He smiles and shows a missing front tooth.

"Oh! Is that man your daddy? Does he ever smile?" Regina looks at the sheriff and sees some amusement and warmth reach his eyes. Finally. "His momma doesn't mind you taking him to apprehend dangerous criminals?" She risks a joke mingled in with her prying into his single status.

"His mom's gone on to glory, ma'am. She has the better portion."

The steadiness in his voice lets Regina know it's been a while since his wife passed. Green light for flirtation. Regina is relentless about some things. Going into her purse, which is bigger than a backpack—she's got issues—she pulls out the gaming console she found in Mary's purse.

"Why don't you use this to vanquish some demons while we ride back to town?"

The boy lurches toward the game, and she pulls it slightly out of his reach. "Is that how you say thank you?"

The little boy straightens up and puts his hands in his lap. "Thank you, ma'am."

Regina smiles and hands him the game system. He turns it on and starts playing with some actual skill, from what Regina can tell, during their ride back. She hopes the best way to a man's heart is through his son.

"Your boy's quite good with that."

"He and I are going to have a little talk later about how he knows to play that game so well. We do our best to deny frivolous technology."

"Life finds a way...are you a Browning native?"

A rich laugh that makes Regina incredibly more interested escapes the sheriff's lips. "Oh, far from it. I came here because of James, like a lot of us. Been here about ten years."

"Ah. A true believer. You just picked up everything and followed the call. I admire that."

The sheriff gives her another long, assessing look. "Not a lot of outsiders get it."

"I get it. You're what the unenlightened," like she was a few hours ago, "call a 'Society man'. That means 'city women' are off the menu. Or does it?"

Jerome, the handsome sheriff, pulls his truck in front of Regina's hotel and walks around to open Regina's door, and she gets out. His son, Jimmy, is immersed in the game.

"If you might ever consider becoming a 'Society girl', then I would be happy to show you what real courtship looks like. It's not modern, but it lasts."

Jerome holds Regina by her shoulders and lowers his head to plant a ground-shaking kiss on her. He pulls one of the twists in her hair.

"Seems you might like it." Stepping back and looking in the car, Jerome holds his hand out to Jimmy. "Party's over. Give Miss Regina back her game."

"Why don't you hold on to that for me? I think my friend would like you to have it. I know I would." It surprises Regina she can form coherent sentences after that kiss, but she presses on to seal the deal.

"Really?" Jimmy's face lights up with pure joy and his smile threatens to split his face in two.

"Regina, you know that's not our way."

She takes a step towards him and puts her finger on his lips. "I won't tell if you won't. Bye, Jerome." Regina focuses on walking seductively into the motel and hopes she succeeds. She notices Jerome stands outside of his truck looking at the motel for a long time. Win.

The door closes behind Regina, and she collapses against it in bewilderment and euphoria. Was that something real or was he just a missionary dater—more interested in converting her than loving her—like Tom Cruise? For all she knew, that's how they kept their numbers strong, by seducing men and women away from the modern world. But it had felt real to her.

"Problem?" Lois, the innkeeper, has been looking at her panting against her front door for the last two minutes.

"The most amazing thing just happened to me."

"Sheriff Jerome Kindle?"

"How do you know?"

"I have eyes and I can look out my own front window. I had a feeling about you two."

"You mean because we're both black?"

"Well, a little. But mostly because he's still looking for something, and I think maybe you are, too."

Looking for something...it reminds Regina that she is supposed to be looking for Mary, and hopefully, finding justice for James Hamerson. She straightens and tries to come to her senses.

"You might be right, but Lois, I have a big favor to ask you on another matter."

Lois looks excited. "Are you working on a new sermon or something? I knew it."

"Something like that. Lois, what size do you wear?"

Secrets and Lies

It is like something from *Little House on the Prairie*, Regina thinks, but she steps out of the inn in an ankle-length denim smock with an honest-to-God bonnet on her head. Walking two blocks over, she makes her way back to the center of town.

She recognizes the cars for the Society of Ageless Wisdom bigwigs because they are sleek, black Escalades that are completely out of place in a modest little town. A man in a driver's uniform of black suit and tie with a black cap holds up a sign that reads "Meredith James." Regina walks up to the man and stands impatiently in front of him until he opens the back door to the truck and lets her in. Then she is whisked away to Society headquarters.

Someone escorts Regina into a hexagon-shaped building that reminds her of the Pentagon. Why make a religious center reminiscent of a building devoted to war? She slips her escort and takes an elevator to the second floor. She steps onto a floor filled with cubicles. Two security guards approach her, and she smiles and walks past them like she knows where she is going.

She slips into an empty cubicle and tries to log onto the computer there. Things are modern enough here, it seems. Her two semesters of computer science did absolutely nothing to help her break into a religious organization's mainframe, exactly as she expects.

Regina spins around in the office chair to face the people who have been looking over her shoulder for the last minute. Her confident smile falters when she sees one is the man she and Sam threw off the train.

"Playtime is over."

She can't see a lump on his head, but she hopes it hurts.

Train man and the two other henchmen take her to the top floor and into a posh office. The chair behind the desk turns around as if a real-life villain is about to explain all the details of their nefarious plan. The chair turning reveals a middle-aged and completely ordinary-looking white man with close-cut brown hair.

"I was wondering who was in charge since James' demise. I figured this was the best way to find out. Let's talk"

"It was your plan to break in here and get caught?"

"I didn't break in! It was just a big misunderstanding. But since I'm here, what do you have to say for yourself? Where in the world is Mary Stammers? What does she have that's so valuable you sent this goon to get it at gunpoint?" Regina turns to the train man. "You do understand that I'm not her now, right?"

The man in charge rubs the back of his neck and suddenly looks tired.

"We were hoping you could tell us where Mary is."

"Why are you trying to find her? What does she have that you want so bad? I'll just bet it has something to do with whatever 'your James' was meeting with Sam Wallers about the night he was shot."

The man in charge and the train man share a glance that lets Regina know she is on the right track. The man thinks for a moment, then pulls a photo out of a drawer and hands it to her. With a cabin and a stream in the background, the photo shows James Hamerson, Mary Stammers, and even that crazy dog posing for the picture. The way their arms wrap around each other says that they are more than friends. So, this was the ex Mary had rekindled things with.

"James was tormented by a demonic spirit that tried to convince him he was a fraud." His words were clipped and monotone.

"Oh, a 'demonic spirit.'" Regina can barely keep from rolling her eyes. "Looks like he couldn't keep his pants zipped. He was supposed to be a family man. Why I bet..."

"While he was being tormented, he compiled a dossier of all the things that those unfamiliar with the Society might see as...problematic."

"And you would rather not be seen as 'problematic?'"

"This entire community is hurting with the loss of our James. A blow like this could finish us."

"I read someone once said the truth will set you free." Regina lets the judgment drip from her words.

"Come off it," the man's average features suddenly became bitter. "You're a minister. You know how this goes. Faith is fragile. Sometimes a stiff breeze can demolish it. I am just trying to protect this flock. Now, you had a rapport with Mary, I understand. Did she give you any idea where she might be and where that electronic dossier James fabricated is?"

Regina is confused. She looks at the picture of James and Mary. Which was the lie? Had his wife and big happy family been a mere convenience that meant little, or had Mary been the thorn in his side, piercing him every time he tried to do good?

"Fabricated? You're saying that 'your James' made up information to put the Society in a poor light? Why?"

"You modern women and your wicked ways. More like Eve than Mary. You are always the downfall of powerful men."

"This isn't Society teaching."

"It wasn't Society teaching. It will be soon."

"A little too eager to pave over your James' legacy, aren't you?"

The man rises and walks to the floor-to-ceiling windows, where he can see much of the town. He gestures to it. "These people, they're like sheep without a shepherd. They need help."

"And you mean to give it to them. The help you think they need."

"You've never had to make tough decisions?"

"I know that sin is sin, and what you're doing feels like a big sin."

"We'll do what we have to. Please, consider helping us."

"I don't know where Mary is. I'm sorry. And I can't say I agree with you about any of this. James Hamerson, at least initially, founded the Society to set people free, not take them captive to lies. Would that make you the father of lies?"

The man's face turns ugly. "Get her out of here. Dump her back in town."

Regina stands and stuffs her hands in the ample pockets of her frock. "I'm ready to leave." She faces the train thug, "Unless you're going to shoot me now."

Regina prays that killing her would bring too much of the attention they are trying to avoid. Train man looks at the man in charge, then looks disappointed as he steps aside to let her pass.

Regina hesitates, then turns back to the man for a moment. "I hope things work out, but not in the way you want."

✳

Exhaustion threatens every step Regina takes to her room at the inn. She finally opens the door, bracing herself to be momentarily overwhelmed by cat figurines and doilies. She is not prepared to see Agent Dellers lounging on her loveseat.

"What part of get on that train and leave town were you unclear about?"

"I'm not in Rocky Mount anymore. I listened. How did you know where I was, anyway?"

Dellers shakes his head. "I'm FBI, and you secured your room with a credit card."

"Well, like I told the head man and his henchmen at the Society, I don't know where Mary is and I don't know where the dossier they're so desperate to find is either."

The expression flickers on Dellers' face. "Of course, we're all very concerned about the dossier." He stands up and paces her room as if he has any right to be there. "Is there any chance you are actually going to leave matters to the professionals?"

"I'll make that determination when I see some professionals."

Dellers looks at her in frustration. "You know, we should be working together. I don't know why you're being difficult. You women and your wicked ways."

"Difficult? I'm looking for Mary!" Regina wonders whether anyone cares about Mary as a person instead of what she represents. It's not fair that murder always throws good sense and tender mercy out the window.

"You are a troublemaker, and if you don't stop messing with things you don't understand, you could tangle with some very powerful men. You won't like that. Your tough girl act won't make it far."

"Tough woman." Regina stands and walks to her door. Opening it, she stares at Dellers in her prompt for him to leave. "You get the idea."

Heading towards the door, Dellers stops and stands too far into Regina's personal space. He wags his finger in her face and gets ready to say something, but just sighs and walks out.

In her room, Regina stares at the cat figurines until she starts to like them. That, and taking slow deep breaths, helps her to process her thoughts and emotions. Looking at the large framed map of Browning that dominates the wall in her room, she notices something. Going into her dress pocket, she retrieves the picture of James, Mary, and the dog she "forgot" to give back to the man at the Society.

"Maybe I *do* know where you are, Mary."

Later that night at a local bridge, two cars idle next to each other. Agent Dellers and the man in charge of the Society are in the middle of a heated argument.

"You're asking an outsider for help? This is not our way. I told you, I have everything under control." Dellers runs a hand over his head in frustration.

"Oh really? If this is you having things under control, I'll have to rethink your usefulness to the Society."

"You had better rethink it. Dossier? Why does some woman from out of town know more about what's at stake here than I do?"

"We were hoping to handle it internally."

"Whatever. Why didn't you tell me?"

"If you had just been able to keep track of Mary, we could have solved both problems at once."

"What's in this dossier she's supposed to have?"

"Fabricated lies that could bring down the Society. It's worth a lot of money and leverage to whoever ends up with it," the man says matter-of-factly as if discussing the weather.

Dellers stares in disbelief. "I thought we were supposed to be working together." He turns away from the man. "Let's just get this done."

"For our James."

Dellers clears his head and turns back to the man. "For our James." He looks out at the water under the bridge. "Where are you, Mary?"

Finding Mary

Bright and early the next morning, Regina buys water, hiking shoes, a large padlock, and the biggest bolt cutter she could find, hoping she can do what she needs without the whole town hearing about it. There's a youngish kid at the register who seems not to be paying much attention, so maybe she has a chance.

She puts her meager fitness to the test by quick-walking out of town towards James' Lot. When she finds an unattended portion of the fence, she takes the metal cutters out of her backpack. Is this the right thing to do? She is about to destroy property when she clips an opening in this fence. She is about to break and enter.

"Lord, help me find Mary...and not wind up behind bars because of it. And give me better options next time, Lord! Like I want to be out here committing crimes. Just cover me. Amen."

She isn't sure she should pray for success in settings like this, but if not now, when?

James' Lot is about five acres, she thinks. Her accuracy depends on her spatial awareness in reading the map in her motel room. It is the only area in Browning that has lots of brooks and streams. That was the clue that had made the penny drop for her. Regina hopes she's right, for Mary's sake, because it's the only lead she has.

It takes her considerable time and muscle to cut through the fence enough to squeeze her way through. Even then, she still tears her clothes. After getting into James' Lot, Regina is relieved to see the land doesn't seem to be patrolled. She relaxes after about a half hour when no one seems to be alerted about the cut in the fence.

Walking deeper into the wooded area, she hopscotches over flowing water and finds everything about the environment incredibly peaceful and invigorating. She could see why Hamerson would have wanted to keep this to himself. Finally reaching the right spot, Taking her picture of Mary, James, and Genghis out of her back pocket, she confirms that the cabin and brook in front of her were the same ones in the photo.

The cabin is a small, three-room unit that is quite the departure for James, who lately was known for spending extravagant amounts of money on his homes. He drove car models so expensive she had never even heard of them. But this is quaint and simple. It speaks of someone who could enjoy life without needing external stimulation. What kind of man had James Hamerson really been? This is where Mary shared on the train she and her ex got back together. Regina was right. It never works out.

She walks up to the cabin and peeks in the front windows, and she steps up to the door. Just then, Regina sees Mary walk around the side of the house. They stare at each other blankly for a moment.

"Regina, thank God you found me! I've been so scared." They share a hug.

"Mary, you don't know how glad I am to see you. You have a lot of explaining to do."

"Regina, you don't know how much I wanted to tell you the whole truth on the train, but I didn't know who to trust. Everything has been upside-down since James died. I barely know whether I'm coming or going."

"Why don't you start at the beginning?"

"Of course. James and I fell in love in college decades ago. It was short but intense. When we met again a few years ago, that same fire and draw were still there, even though he was married with kids and the leader of the Society. It had always been James for me, so what could I do? After fighting it for a long time, we started meeting here. It reminded us about the place in upstate New York we used to sneak into off-season.

"I was in DC with James when he decided to meet with that reporter. He just wanted out. He was going to leave the Society and his wife and it was finally going to be just him and I. Sam called to tell James he was running late to their meeting, but James had already left. I went after him to tell him to wait. I walked over there with my dog, Genghis. That's when I saw him get shot, right in front of me."

Mary broke into tears, and Regina comforted her.

"But why was he giving Sam damaging information to bring down the Society?"

"What? Who told you that, Henry?"

"Henry?"

"The bland-faced man who wants to run the Society. He knew James was going to walk away from it all ,and Henry could see his own future going up in flames. James would never bring down the Society. It was his creation. He just wanted to be free."

"So then, what is this dossier that the Society wants back? They're pretty terrified of it if they would try to enlist my help in trying to find it."

"James found out that some of his most trusted people in the work were committing crimes made possible by their positions and access. He had info that would cleanse the Society, not destroy it. The information is probably about Henry, so of course he would say something like that. You see how I don't know who I can trust?"

"It is hard to tell who the good guy is here, I'll admit. Why didn't you tell the FBI that you and James were seeing each other?"

"The Society's reach goes everywhere. I couldn't be sure it wouldn't get back to Henry. For all I know, they were the ones who shot James. And that's why I had to get off the train, Regina. I *saw* the man who shot James! I knew he was there for me, so I just ran. I went to the last place I really felt safe. This space was just for us."

"It's difficult to tell whose side anybody is on. If you don't know who to trust, there's somebody I trust. Will you come with me to meet my friend, Reverend Croning? He has ties to the Justice Department. I'm supposed to be preaching at his church for revival tomorrow night."

"I suppose I can't keep going like I'm going. Yes, I'll do it."

"Do you have a car? We could drive and stay off of the radar that way. Don't worry, we'll get this all sorted out."

"Thank you. I appreciate you," Mary says. "How did you even find me, anyway?"

Regina pulls out the picture of the happy couple and dog and hands it to her. "I figured out that this was where the train stopped. I saw a map of Browning and then remembered what you had said about the cabin and your ex. I thought James' Lot might be your meeting place."

"Oh. How clever." She fingers the picture in a quiet moment. "How is Genghis?"

"The ancient conqueror and philanderer?"

"No, my dog." She points to him in the picture. "He was also on the train."

"Oh, yes! I met him in the cargo compartment. I've got to tell you, he's terrifying."

"He is like that with strangers, but he wasn't like that with me, or with James. He is fiercely protective of and as gentle as a lamb with the people he loves."

The noise of a car pulling up to the cabin hits both of their ears at once. Mary jumps up in fear.

"Please tell me you're expecting someone, Regina."

Regina wonders if she's been caught. Has Sheriff Jerome, or worse, Henry, found her? She edges towards a front-facing window and peers out. It's another man from the train! She thought he had been wearing a holstered gun as he followed Mary out of the dining car. He approaches the cabin and pulls out his gun.

"We need to go."

Thankfully, the cabin had a back door. They exit and leave the man in their dust.

"I just want to bring you back under our protection!" The man doubts they hear him.

He makes a call. "Found Sarah, but they're on the run now. Her and the lady from the train. I'll transmit the vehicle details..." His head drops. "Yes, I know I had one job. I know I'm on thin ice. Why do you think I'm working so hard to fix things...yes, sir. I'm on it."

He has no idea he's being played, but one thing he does know—if that thin ice breaks, it's over for him. He has to catch them before his streak of bad luck gets a lot worse.

Spun Like a Top

They split the driving into three-hour shifts and the miles fly by. Regina pulls into another gas station for them to fill up and take a bathroom break.

"Alright, time to switch. You ready to drive?" Regina turns off the car and looks for the lever to open the gas cap. "We're almost in Miami. This last stretch ought to get us there. I've got to tell you, I'll be glad to close this chapter."

"Me too. And thank you, you've been so nice. I wish I could pay you back, or even do something like pay for gas, but I left my purse on the train. Do you still have my purse?"

"Oh, yes, of course. It's in my luggage that went on with the train. Pastor Croning arranged to have it picked up for me." Regina hopes her lie comes out natural and believable. "And don't worry about the gas. You pump, I'll pay."

In line for the gas cashier, Regina grabs some cash from her wallet, then hesitates. She uses her credit card instead. "Can you add a lottery ticket? Random numbers, thanks." Won't it be funny if she wins, she thinks.

When she returns, she sees Mary slip a screwdriver into the glove compartment.

"Is everything alright?"

Fastening her seat belt, Mary starts the car and gives Regina a smile. "It will be. Just a little insurance."

A few hours later, they pull into the parking lot of Redeemer Nondenominational Church and find an open spot near the entrance. It's one of those big mega churches, and the steepled, three-story building is stunning as it sits in the middle of a large parking lot. Palm trees line the walkway and everything looks immaculate.

They get out and better appreciate the structure. It makes her medium-sized church look like a shack in comparison. Regina and Mary go inside and the friendly staff greet them. They let Regina know that Pastor Croning will arrive shortly. They let them look at the sanctuary, normally closed on nights with no service, seeing as Regina will preach there tomorrow.

When they enter, her jaw drops. It is massive and looks like it can easily seat a thousand. Opportunities to preach in settings like this don't come every day, Regina knows.

"Thank you, God." she breathes out a prayer.

Regina catches movement in the corner and turns to find the man that had found them at James' Lot approaching her.

"If you brought a gun into this sanctuary, you need to think carefully about what you do next. I would leave it in the holster if I were you."

He laughs. "I'm the one with the power here, but you sound like you're warning me. I'd be more afraid if I were you."

"Oh, I'm terrified. Just not of you. You should be afraid, too." Regina nods her head, and Mary pops out from a pew and knocks over the man. Regina holds her backpack over his groin and drops it. While he clutches his family jewels, she disarms him.

She has never held a firearm before. Regina can't believe such a small thing could take every life in this building. She can't bring herself to point it at the man, especially in God's sanctuary.

"Harder than it looks, isn't it?" The man winces as he slowly gets to his feet.

"You have very poor peripheral awareness, especially for a federal agent." Regina hopes her guess is correct.

"You know who I am? Then why have you been running?"

"Because I know who you are."

"What?"

"Why should I feel safe around the FBI? And why should she?"

"So you drive to a church? How's that going to help you?"

Agent Dellers walks in with a full complement of federal and, by the looks of it, state law enforcement. He walks up to Regina and holds out a hand for the gun.

"Were you not afraid to approach me? I was armed." Regina's voice is shaky now that she is relieved of the gun and can take a free breath again.

"I figured you would have shot me on site if you wanted to. Plus, if I don't miss my guess, you called me here."

"Yup."

The agent from the train and Mary both look at her. "What?" They say in unison.

"I used my credit card and even bought lottery tickets to tip you off. I figured you might want to nab to person who murdered James Hamerson."

Mary nods her head and points to the man from the train. "Yes, he shot James."

Regina shakes her head from side-to-side, and Dellers looks at Mary funny. "That's the agent we assigned to you on the train. We didn't tell you so that you wouldn't give him away. He works out of our North Carolina field office." Dellers turns to Regina. "Did you lead me on a wild goose chase for this nonsense? I hope you did not waste my time."

"He's not the murderer. She is." Regina gestures her head in Mary's direction.

"*Sarah?*" Dellers looks incredulous.

"Who? Oh, yes. Mary, Sarah, *her*."

"You're gonna have to explain this one to me."

"She and James Hamerson were seeing each other. That's part of the story Sam Wallers was hoping to crack. The other part was going to bring the Society to its knees, whether rightly or wrongly, I don't know."

"Wait. What do you mean 'seeing each other?' James is married."

"Is infidelity new? He was committing it." She hands him the picture of James and Mary in front of the cabin.

Dellers takes the photo, and his face blanches.

"Yet another thing Henry didn't tell you, I take it?"

"What?"

"You and him are in cahoots, I figure. How else would he have known it was me in Browning? And you both use the same terminology when talking about us wicked women bringing down virtuous men or some dribble like that."

Dellers shakes his head as if he could rid himself of this meddlesome priest. He takes a breath to stay focused. "If Sarah was having an affair with our James, why would she kill him?"

Regina tries not to act surprised to find out Dellers was a Society man. She had thought perhaps he might be a sympathizer, but only believers said 'our James' the same way other religions revere their founders.

"She loved him and the money the Society provided." Regina turned to face Mary. "That's how you know Henry, right? If James destroyed what he created, where would her fortune be then?"

Dellers turned so that only Regina could see him. "That all you got? Pretty weak sauce."

Inwardly, Regina is crushed. He doesn't like the first part of her theory, but she presses on. "We can all agree that James had the dossier on him when he was shot." Heads nodded. "Then why did the Society's henchman threaten me at gunpoint for the dossier, thinking that I was her? Why would she have it unless she had gotten it from James' body? And more importantly—Genghis."

Sarah shook her head. "What *about* my dog in this ridiculous theory of yours?"

"You said, the night you saw James die, that you went out with Genghis to find him and tell him Sam was going to be late. You told me he was very protective of you and James. Why didn't he attack the killer then?"

Dellers turns around and raises an inquisitive eyebrow at Sarah.

"I don't know what is in this dossier, but you decided it was worth killing the leader of the Society for Ageless Wisdom on the steps of my church."

"What?" Sarah and Dellers say in unison.

"The steps of my church. You and Genghis followed James as he went to meet Sam Wallace to let the truth come to light. But the police responded so quickly you couldn't get away. You posed as a witness, someone who just happened to be passing by when he got shot. That's why Dellers didn't know you knew James, because if he knew, you would become the suspect.

"Now that you had the dossier, you had to sell it to get that life you've always wanted. The only time you would have enough wiggle room from your federal protection detail was on the train. You left your purse at the dinner table. That was the drop. But it was never completed because I picked it up and tried to find you to give it back.

"When we were on the way here, you asked me if I still had your purse. How would you know I might have your purse unless the buyers had seen me pick it up that night and told you? You ransacked your own room, then pulled the emergency stop on the train when you were near Browning and went where you thought you'd lie low for a while.

"You were surprised to see me, that was for sure. But you knew you had a chance to get your dossier back and salvage your plan. I fell for your entire story—hook, line, and sinker. We pulled a Thelma and Louise or something driving down to Florida. You never once corrected me when I kept calling you Mary. That's when I knew the truth was 'fluid' for you. Then, when you asked me about the purse, I knew.

"Now you don't have your man or your money. Was it worth it?"

Sarah looks at her in disbelief, shakes her head, and laughs. "You can't prove any of that."

"I've heard enough," Dellers interrupts. "You and I are going to have a much longer conversation now that all this has come to light. Take her in for questioning."

Agents step forward and take a dazed Sarah Stammers into custody.

Agent Dellers turns back to Regina and gives her an impressed, assessing look, lingering over her curves as he takes stock of her. "I don't suppose..." He lets the question hang in the air.

"Yeah, no. Now, what are we going to do about the buyers?" Regina is eager to wrap things up.

"Who?"

"The buyers of the dossier."

"Dossier? There is no dossier." Dellers' face is the picture of ignorance.

"But what about Sam Wallers? Don't you see? Sarah was already off the train when he got shot. It must have been the buyers thinking he had it because he had been in Sarah's room. We have to find them."

"I don't care about any dossier on some memory card, and I don't care about Sam. I've caught my murderer, and I've gotten our James some justice. That's enough for me." He starts to walk away, then turns back. "Let's never meet again."

The agent from the train loitered behind the other retreating agents and officers. "I'm Ramirez. Thanks for finding the witness, well, I guess the killer, for us. For me. She went missing on my watch. That could have been my career. The only leads I had were from following you."

"Did Agent Dellers say he didn't care about a dossier on a memory chip?"

"Yes, why?"

"I think I know where it is. You and I have got to get back to Browning."

"What? I can't get authorization for that." Ramirez stops, puts his hands on his hips, and stares at the floor for a minute. "You've been right so far. Let's do it."

"Alright. Justice Team: deploy!" Regina raises her hand for a high five and Ramirez leaves her hanging. Some people are no fun.

Twist the Knife

Regina fidgets with her phone as the plane taxies the runway toward their arrival gate.

"Nobody's picking up at the sheriff's office. I need to warn him."

"Gonna tell me what this is about yet?" Ramirez drums his fingers on the armrest.

"Not yet. Don't quite trust you." She delivers the statement in a sing-song voice.

Ramirez wonders if Regina is one of those idiot savants.

A couple hours after landing, they pull on to Browning's Main Street. Regina's phone rings, and she drops it like a hot potato.

"Hello?"

"I hear you've been moving heaven and earth trying to find me. I knew you couldn't stay away."

"Jerome, please tell me Jimmy is with you."

"No. Why?"

"Do you have the gaming system I gave him? Is it with you?"

"No, he has it. What is this about?"

"I'm back in town on Main Street. We have to find Jimmy and that console. I may have inadvertently put him in danger."

"He should be at baseball practice. I'll go there, you slow drive in a grid, in case he went somewhere else."

The call ends.

On a park bench, Jimmy sits and plays his gaming system. A car at the end of the block slowly approaches so quietly, Jimmy doesn't even notice. He is going to be an easy target for them, stationary and inattentive. The silencer is put on the gun, and a hand extends out of the driver's window, taking aim.

A car comes screeching to a halt between the gun and the boy. Ramirez leaps out and draws his weapon as he yells commands at the car. The gun with the silencer is dropped, and it matches Regina's jaw.

"Mr. and Mrs. Palmer?"

"Oh, hi dear. How are you?" The man starts to put his hands down until Ramirez reminds him to hold them high. Mrs. Palmer is sitting in the passenger seat, looking like she's confused about why their leisurely drive has been interrupted.

"*You* were buying the dossier on the Society for Ageless Wisdom? Why?"

"Our daughter left us for the Society. She was wandering through life as a young adult and they preyed on her hunger and need for purpose. Turned her into a Society girl. Moved her to this damn town. She cut off all ties to us, saying that's her old life. We've tried for years, but all the begging was worth nothing.

"I thought if we could get the dossier and show her the truth, she might come back to us."

"And you were gonna shoot this kid to make that happen?"

Tears fill his eyes. "Well, he's one of them, ain't he?"

"That little boy is God's joy, and so is your daughter. They deserve to live full lives, both of them. I'm sorry your relationship with your daughter is damaged, but I hope you know this is not right."

He starts to cry, and the woman drops her head.

Regina walks over to Ramirez. "They were gonna shoot that kid."

"Sure looked that way to me."

"So I suppose we can't let them go, huh?"

Ramirez keeps his gun trained on the Palmers but spares her a glance. "Oh no, don't you get started with that forgive and forget crap. What about your buddy Sam from the train? I bet ballistics from that gun will match his gunshot wound."

"I wasn't going to say forgive and forget!" Regina deflates. "It just seems really sad. But you're right, we all have to pay for what we take, in this world or the next."

"We'll understand it better, by and by."

A slow smile comes to Regina's lips as she recognizes the words to the title of one of her grandmother's favorite hymns. "Are you Christian?"

It surprises Regina that she got so wrapped up in the drama she is just now noticing Agent Ramirez isn't wearing a wedding ring. It could just be because he's working on a case, though.

"Not really, just remember it was something my grandmother used to sing."

"Mine too." They share a moment.

Sheriff Jerome clears his throat behind them.

Ramirez gets busy agent-ing, or whatever FBI men do. Sheriff Jerome and his deputy help take them into custody and take care of getting their car towed as evidence. He also explains to Jimmy that he can't keep the gaming console because it's very important evidence for justice.

Finally, they have a moment, somewhat, to themselves. Regina turns toward Jerome. He's holding his son, who's asleep and looking so cute she wants to run off with just the boy, which is saying something, given how fine Sheriff Jerome has been looking, being in command of the scene.

"So...what's up?" Regina sometimes runs out of witty repartee.

"Agent Ramirez, hmmm?"

"Jealous?"

"Yes."

Regina does not expect his honesty.

"I'll drop him," she replies without even thinking.

Jerome gives her a long look that she can't interpret. He takes a step back. "A man named Henry came to see me. Apparently, he's high up in the Society, though I don't know him well. They are looking for a new face of the Society since we've lost our James. He wants it to be me. Something about elevating ordinary, everyday faith. It's an incredible opportunity. My life does need to be above reproach, though."

Regina's heart plummets. "And I'm reproach, right? You need a modern woman minister from another tradition like you need a millstone around your neck." Regina shakes herself out of her sadness. "I get it. It's not like I was going to give up everything and wear frocks and bonnets," she lies. She might have, maybe her cell phone ran her life a little too much, anyway. Now she will never have the chance to find out what decision she would have made.

"This is difficult for me, but I have the chance to make a real difference for the faith. Our people are hurting so much right now. I have to do all that I can, no matter how much I would like things to be different."

"Just please don't get played. Henry is a weasel."

"You think it's that easy to play me?"

"I don't know what kind of man James Hamerson was when he began, but he seemed to be something really different by the end, to the detriment of him and the movement he started. I don't want that to happen to you."

"I'll do my best. Really. Thanks for saving Jimmy. If you had been a little later..."

She waves away the thanks. "It was the least I could do. I really do hope you help make the Society something more like what James first dreamed it could be."

Her eyes want to explode with tears, and she has to get out of Sheriff Jerome's presence as soon as possible, but she is rooted to the spot.

"Well, I'll leave you be. Just wanted to let you know where things stand with me." He gets in his truck, gives her a last look, and drives away.

Regina woodenly walks to the bench Jimmy had been sitting on and bawls her eyes out. Ramirez leaves her to her tears. Anyone with eyes could see she needed a minute. Finally, she dries her eyes, takes a few deep breaths, and stands up, determined to feel better.

"I've still got a sermon to write."

She is not embarrassed to drive back to the airport with Ramirez because no woman no cry. She flies back to Miami, and will either write the sermon of her life or not. She won't know until tomorrow when it's time to preach it.

Amen

1,213 people—she knew because mega churches have automated people-counting software monitoring the sanctuary entrances—sing and clap to the praise music as Regina sits in the pulpit of Redeemer Nondenominational Church in Miami, Florida next to her father in the ministry, Pastor Croning.

If someone had a dossier on him, would she do whatever it took to cover it up? Had they come to rely too much on the whiz-bang of technology instead of the timeless principles of the faith? Did 'our James' have it right, at least in the beginning? Had she just been driven to meddle in James' murder because of her own insecurities and doubts? She is thinking about anything but the sermon she is supposed to deliver in mere minutes.

Before she knows it, she's up and at the pulpit. A congregation that has been taught to revere the Word of God is waiting for her to preach. She looks at the faces in the congregation and knows that they are going in the right direction. This is the work they are meant to be doing.

She sees same-sex couples who feel free to be themselves and worship their God in an atmosphere of welcome and affirmation. She sees a mix of generations and cultures. She sees homeless and down-on-their-luck folks sprinkled in the crowd and no one is shying away from them. Actually, they look like they're waiting for her to speak.

"Any time, Rev."

Regina plays off her extended pause. "Come, let us worship the Lord in the beauty of holiness." The crowd goes for it.

"Now, Lawd knows life for me ain't been no crystal staircase—maybe not for some of you, either—but we are still charged to live our lives to the best of our abilities. Every choice we make adds up to equal our character. Just because you start out virtuous and perfect, or so you think, doesn't mean you will stay that way. So, I urge you to make the right choices—day by day, over and over. Sometimes we just don't know what the right thing is, and then we need to pray more, but most of the time, you know.

"Do the *right* thing. Not the acceptable thing, not the defensible act, not even sometimes the legal thing. Because, whether or not you recognize it, someone is always counting and depending on you. Maybe someone is desperate for justice. Maybe someone has lost their way and just needs someone to be understood. Maybe someone has to be held accountable. Maybe that someone will even be you sometime.

"Now with that off of my chest, let's turn to our text for the night..."

Late the next afternoon, Regina walks into the main office at Methuen Baptist Church.

"Good preach, Pastor. Caught the stream last night. You certainly were in your glory."

"Wrote it on the plane that afternoon."

"Get out! Why so last minute, more extracurricular activities? Reverend Croning called and said you had gotten off the train early."

"You know me. I'm always getting into something. It's a wonder my guardian angel hasn't retired yet. The stories they could tell."

If she only knew.

www.ingramcontent.com/pod-product-compliance
Lightning Source LLC
Chambersburg PA
CBHW070648130626
46555CB00006B/2763